P9-ECY-488

OSSIRON
THE FLESHLESS KILLER

WITHDRAWN

BY ADAM BLADE

ORCHARD

With special thanks to Tabitha Jones

www.beastquest.co.uk

ORCHARD BOOKS

First published in Great Britain in 2022 by The Watts Publishing Group

1 3 5 7 9 10 8 6 4 2

Text © Beast Quest Limited 2022
Cover and inside illustrations by Steve Sims
© Beast Quest Limited 2022

Beast Quest is a registered trademark of Beast Quest Limited
Series created by Beast Quest Limited, London

The moral rights of the author and illustrator have been asserted.
All characters and events in this publication, other than those clearly in the public domain,
are fictitious and any resemblance to real persons, living or dead, is purely coincidental.

All rights reserved.
No part of this publication may be reproduced, stored in a retrieval system, or transmitted, in any form
or by any means, without the prior permission in writing of the publisher, nor be otherwise circulated in
any form of binding or cover other than that in which it is published and without a similar condition
including this condition being imposed on the subsequent purchaser.

A CIP catalogue record for this book is available from the British Library.

ISBN 978 1 40836 536 6

Printed in Great Britain

The paper and board used in this book are made from wood from responsible sources.

Orchard Books
An imprint of Hachette Children's Group
Part of The Watts Publishing Group Limited
Carmelite House, 50 Victoria Embankment, London EC4Y 0DZ

An Hachette UK Company
www.hachette.co.uk
www.hachettechildrens.co.uk

Welcome to the world of Beast Quest!

Tom was once an ordinary village boy, until he travelled to the City, met King Hugo and discovered his destiny. Now he is the Master of the Beasts, sworn to defend Avantia and its people against Evil. Tom draws on the might of the magical Golden Armour, and is protected by powerful tokens granted to him by the Good Beasts of Avantia. Together with his loyal companion Elenna, Tom is always ready to visit new lands and tackle the enemies of the realm.

While there's blood in his veins, Tom will never give up the Quest...

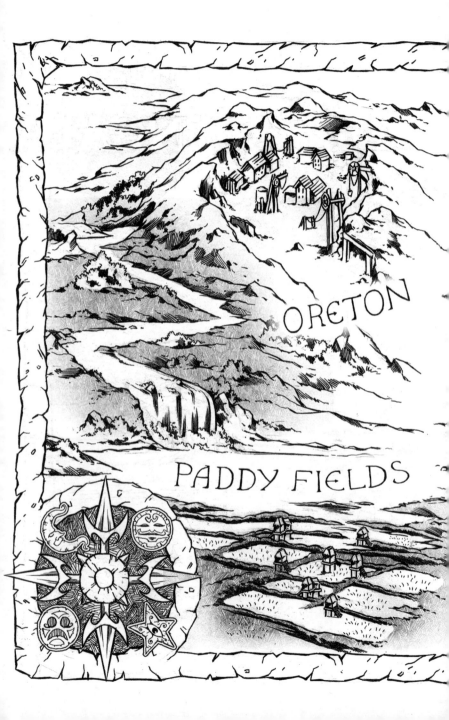

ORETON

PADDY FIELDS

There are special gold coins to collect in this book. You will earn one coin for every chapter you read.

Find out what to do with your coins at the end of the book.

CONTENTS

You thought I was gone, did you not? Swallowed by the Netherworld, never to set foot in the upper world again... Consumed by the Beasts that roam this foul place... Well, it's not that easy to be rid of the most powerful magician who ever stalked the land.

I have the perfect plan up my sleeve, and soon I shall leave this Realm of Beasts behind.

And the best part? My arch enemy Tom will die in the process.

See you all very soon!

Malvel

TRIALS IN TANGALA

A cloudless sky arched over Tangala's capital, Pania, and the sunlight glinted off the pointed spires of Queen Aroha's palace.

The day of the Trials had finally arrived and, judging by the packed benches all around him, Tom thought half of Tangala must have

come to watch. He craned forward
in his front-row seat between
Elenna and Daltec, trying to get a
better view of the contestants he
and Elenna had helped select. The
brave hopefuls waited in a fenced
enclosure just off the main arena.
Some were practising their moves,
jabbing and thrusting their
weapons. Others were limbering up
or polishing their armour.

The contestants had travelled from
all over Tangala to try out for the
title of Master or Mistress of the
Beasts. Men and women. Young and
old. All willing to risk their lives to
protect Tangala. Tom was pleased
to see many of the applicants were

young people. He and Elenna had insisted the contest should be open to all. After all, they knew better than anyone that heroes could come from humble beginnings.

Turning his attention to the tiered benches of spectators, Tom spotted cat-people from Viga sitting alongside fisherfolk and forest dwellers, desert people and those from the mountain clans, all laughing and chatting as they waited for the Trials to begin.

Street vendors weaved between the rows, selling roasted nuts and candied fruit, while in the main arena a band played a raucous song about the brave Masters of the

Beasts of the past.

"I wasn't sure about all this pomp and ceremony," Elenna said, leaning in close to Tom. "But I have to admit, Rotu's done a great job!"

After a series of Beast attacks on Tangala, Queen Aroha had asked her nephew Prince Rotu to find two new heroes to protect the kingdom. Tom and Elenna had been drafted in to select the candidates, while the prince focussed on his own area of expertise: the entertainment.

"It's good to see the people enjoying themselves after everything that's happened," Tom said.

"And Aroha's definitely made the right choice!" Daltec added. "You and Elenna can't be in two places at once, which means Tangala definitely needs its own Master of the Beasts!"

A gong sounded from the far side of the arena where Prince Rotu sat on a raised dais, his gold-and-silver dress armour gleaming in the sun. He lifted a hand and the music faded, an expectant hush falling over the crowd.

"Let the first contestants come forward!" Rotu cried.

Four participants – all younger than Tom – hurried from their fenced enclosure and into the main arena. *I hope they all do well!* Each walked with their head held high, but their faces were solemn and pinched with nerves as the hopefuls took up their places before the prince.

"I'm glad we never had to do this," Elenna whispered.

"Me too," Tom said. He knew that many of the contestants would never even have set foot in Pania before, let alone been addressed by royalty.

Rotu pointed to the first contender, a tall, lithe girl with choppy dark hair and a serious look in her eyes. "Introduce yourself," he said.

The girl bowed low, then took a massive axe from a belt at her waist. "I am Katya," she said, tossing the axe from hand to hand, as if

it weighed
nothing at
all. "I come
from the
Forest of
Shadows. I
pledge my
axe to you,
and to all
of Tangala."

"Well said," Rotu said, nodding
with approval. Then he turned to
the next contestant in line – a wiry
boy with brown skin and a patch
over one eye. The boy held out a
gleaming, long-handled scythe and
bowed to the prince.

"Nolan of Aran," the boy said. "My

scythe is yours to command."

Rotu smiled. "Thank you."

Next, a slight girl with dark skin and fierce brown eyes stepped forward. In one hand she held a trident taller than her, and in the other, a fishing net. She dropped into a curtsy.

"I am honoured to meet you," the girl told Rotu. "I come from the western shore. My family fish the ocean, but we are renowned as warriors too. My name is Miandra. I promise you now that while there's breath in my body, I shall defend my kingdom."

Elenna nudged Tom, grinning. "She's clearly learned from a

master!" she whispered. Tom couldn't help returning the smile.

In the arena, Rotu turned to the last of the four contestants – a stocky boy with a shock of fair hair. He was wearing a leather apron and held a blacksmith's hammer. "And, finally, can you tell me a little about yourself?" Rotu asked.

The boy had been looking at his feet, but now made an awkward bow, blushing fiercely as he met the prince's gaze.

"Rafe," the boy said, his voice gruff but clear. "I am a blacksmith like my father and his father before him, but I would rather use my hammer to defend Tangala, if I can."

"Wonderful!" Rotu said, beaming. "A blacksmith's boy, like Tom." The

prince's gaze swept across all four contestants. "Now, let the Trials begin!"

As four of Aroha's fiercest warrior women strode into the arena, a dark shadow passed over Tom, momentarily blocking the sun. He looked up to see a large red-and-blue bird sailing across the courtyard – it was bigger than an eagle but had the same cruel, curved beak and taloned feet.

"What's that bird?" Tom whispered to Daltec, pointing as it landed on the far wall of the courtyard. "I've never seen one like it."

"A Janus bird," Daltec said, frowning. "They are rare in any kingdom, and I have never seen one here. They are magical birds, able to cross between realms."

"I hope it's not a bad omen," Elenna said, narrowing her eyes as she gazed at the creature.

Tom loosened his sword in its sheath. "Let's be on our guard, just in case," he said, then turned his attention back to the contest.

Aroha's warriors were taking up position opposite the four young candidates. The muscular women, each wielding a longsword and shield, dwarfed their opponents. But Tom knew size and age could be deceptive.

"Let the sparring begin!" Rotu cried.

A mighty cheer rose from the crowd. Aroha's four warriors struck a combative stance, and the candidates lifted their weapons to more excited chanting and cheers.

"*SQUAAAAWK!*" The screech ripped through the noise of the crowd, jerking Tom's gaze up just in time to see the Janus bird make a low swoop overhead.

BOOM! The whole courtyard lurched, jolting Tom's body and almost throwing him from his seat. The crowd's joyful cheers turned to terrified screams, and thick clouds of dust filled the air. Crashes and bangs rang out all around Tom as the tiered benches started to collapse. He tried to stand, but the flagstones were shaking so much he could barely stay upright.

"An earthquake!" Elenna shouted.

TOM'S OLDEST ENEMY

Screaming people fled in every direction, staggering and lurching over the quaking ground. Tom's first thought was for Rotu, but peering through the dust, he saw Aroha's trained warriors already hurrying towards the prince.

CRACK! A tremendous splitting

sound echoed through the courtyard as more plumes of dust erupted upwards.

"We're trapped!" A powerful young voice rose above the din. Tom recognised it instantly. *Miandra!*

The dust swirled, clearing enough for Tom to spot the four candidates. They were stranded on an island of shuddering ground in the middle of the arena, each trying to help the others stay upright. The flagstones seemed to have split open around them, creating a chasm too wide to jump. With a jolt of alarm, Tom realised the small island where the young warriors stood was crumbling too!

Tom launched himself towards them. As he raced over the quaking ground, he summoned a mental image of his suit of magical armour, stored safely back in Avantia. Calling on the power of his golden boots, he felt a rush of energy surge into his legs, giving him the strength he would need to leap the chasm...

But before Tom was close enough to jump, Miandra yelped. Her eyes widened in shock as the ground beneath her gave way. Katya grabbed Miandra's tunic, steadying her for a moment, but then she too overbalanced and both fell, plummeting into the void. Rafe and Nolan reached out, trying to catch

hold of the girls, but the remaining flagstones crumbled, and they vanished too. Tom heard Nolan call out, but his voice was cut off in mid-shout.

Tom reached the edge of the crater as the earth gave one last shudder then fell still. He looked down to see a swirling mass of glowing green-and-purple vapour. There was no sign of the four candidates – or of the bottom of the hole. *A portal!* Tom realised. He bent his knees, ready to leap in, but strong hands gripped his shoulders from behind. Tom glanced back to see Daltec and Elenna holding him.

"That portal could lead anywhere!" Daltec said.

"I know!" Tom cried. "It will take me wherever the candidates went! I have to go after them!" But, as he said the words, the ground gave another lurch and the hole at his feet snapped shut like the jaws of a Beast. Tom's shoulders sagged. It was too late. The four brave young heroes were gone.

Tom, Elenna and Daltec all hurried to the throne room, where they found Prince Rotu pacing up and down. He was still wearing his dress armour, and spun to face them as soon as they entered.

"What a disastrous start to a tournament!" Rotu said. "Daltec, where could our young competitors have gone?"

Daltec rubbed his chin, frowning. "I have a feeling the portal must have something to do with the Janus bird that Tom and I spotted. They are able to travel freely between realms – but I've never heard of them taking others with them."

The wizard drew a glass orb from his cloak and cradled it in his palm. "I should be able to find them easily enough…" he said, gazing into the crystal. The ball was smaller than the one Daltec usually used in Avantia, and Tom had to crowd in close beside Elenna to see. Daltec spoke a few guttural words, then passed his free hand over the surface of the crystal. The ball quickly filled with a swirling green-and-purple mist.

"That's it!" Tom said, feeling hopeful. "That's the same mist that I saw in the portal."

Daltec shook his head, frowning.

"It's some sort of smokescreen," he said. "Someone is blocking my magic. Someone powerful. I can't—" Daltec gave a yelp and almost dropped the ball as a face suddenly appeared, staring right up at them out of the crystal.

Tom's blood went icy cold as he took in lank grey hair, a sharp nose and cruel, piercing eyes the colour of pond slime. The face looking back at them was one he knew far too well. *Malvel!*

"No…" Elenna breathed.

"Yes!" Malvel hissed. Then he let out a long, hideous cackle. The Dark Wizard looked haggard and gaunt, with hollow cheeks and sunken eyes.

His green hood was ragged, and his hands, closed around a thick, leather-bound book, were chapped and stained with dirt.

"How can he have survived?" Elenna asked.

Tom couldn't speak. The last time he had seen Malvel, the villain was falling through a rift in reality, into the Netherworld – a deadly realm filled with murderous Beasts.

"The *Book of Derthsin*," Daltec

muttered. "He must have used its magic to control the Beasts."

Malvel cleared his throat noisily. "Excuse me!" he snapped, his eyes narrowing. "I'm here to make a bargain."

"What have you done with our candidates?" Tom growled back.

"Oh, they're quite safe," Malvel said breezily. "I have no intention of killing them…yet. They're being guarded by my Beasts. If you wish to see them alive again, my price is very modest. All I need is your purple jewel. Give it to the Janus bird, and I will return the children." Tom heard a squawk from outside the open window and glanced up to see the red-and-blue bird alight on the sill. It cocked its head and fixed Tom with a steady yellow gaze.

Tom turned back to the crystal. "I do not make bargains," he said. "Nor will I allow my magical tokens to fall into the wrong hands. I'll find the contestants myself, and I'll free them. While there is blood in my veins, the jewel will never be yours!"

Malvel let out a long sigh. "Oh, how I have missed hearing that quaint little phrase of yours," he said. "And the way you always seem to think you have a choice..." Malvel's face hardened. "I will tell you one last time," he spat. "Give me the jewel, or you will never see those pitiful runts again!"

CROSSING OVER

Tom tore his gaze from Malvel's hideous scowl and glanced up at Elenna and Daltec. Both looked pale and stricken.

"He'll never keep his word," Elenna said.

"No," Daltec agreed. "And if he gets hold of the purple jewel, he'll be able to create a portal and escape from the Netherworld."

Tom clenched his jaw. "Then how do we stop him?"

"You *can't* stop me!" Malvel shouted from the crystal ball. "That's what I've been trying to tell you. So, save us all some time and hand over the jewel!"

"Never!" Tom vowed.

Malvel sighed again. "Those innocent children will pay for your obstinacy. And once I find a way out of here, so shall you!" The wizard's glowering image vanished abruptly, leaving a haze of green-and-purple mist. From its perch on the sill, the Janus bird let out a raucous shriek. Tom looked up to see it flap its wings and fly away.

"Stop that bird!" Daltec cried suddenly. "It might be our only hope of saving the candidates."

Tom dashed to the window with Elenna at his side, ready to leap

after the creature. But he could see he was already too late. The bird was flying towards a shimmering green-and-purple portal in the sky.

"Maybe I can clip its wing," Elenna said. She lifted her bow and fired an arrow. It whizzed through the air, catching the tip of the bird's wing. To Tom's dismay, the bird didn't slow. Instead, it let out an angry squawk and flapped through the portal, which instantly vanished. A single red feather spiralled slowly to the ground.

"I'm sorry," Elenna said, hanging her head.

"No," Daltec said from just behind them. "You did brilliantly."

"How so?" Tom asked.

"Every feather of the Janus bird carries the essence of its magic," Daltec said. "It's not strictly allowed

– and the Circle of Wizards will be furious if they find out – but I can use this feather to make another portal."

Tom's heart leapt. *There's still hope!*

A short while later, once Tom had collected the feather from the courtyard and one of Rotu's aides had found a pestle and mortar for Daltec, they all gathered in the throne room once more.

Daltec looked as solemn as Tom had ever seen him. "Now, you must realise that once you are on the other side, you are on your own,"

Daltec said. "This portal will close and you will have to find your own way back using the purple jewel."

"I understand," Elenna said.

Tom nodded. "We'll be back. And we'll bring all four candidates with us."

"The sooner the better if you can, otherwise I'll have some difficult explaining to do!" Rotu said.

Daltec placed the Janus bird's bright red feather into the mortar. Then he closed his eyes and clicked his fingers above the dish. The feather instantly burst into sizzling blue flames that crackled and spat. Daltec muttered an incantation, his hands hovering over

the small fire. Blue smoke began
to pour from the spitting crucible,
billowing upwards and outwards
to form an opaque wall. Reams and
reams of it kept coming, until it
formed a rectangle as tall as Tom
that reached all the way to the floor.

Finally, Daltec lowered his hands, pursed his lips and blew into the smoke. The centre of the rectangle cleared, creating a doorway big enough for Tom and Elenna to step through. On the other side Tom could see the same swirling green-and-purple vapour that the candidates had vanished into.

Tom drew his sword. "Ready?" he asked Elenna.

"Always," Elenna said.

"Wait a moment!" Daltec commanded. Then he clicked his fingers again. A rolled parchment appeared in his hand. He passed it to Tom. "You'll need a map."

"Thank you," Tom said.

"Don't thank me until you've seen it," Daltec replied with a rueful smile. "As maps go, it's not the most reliable." Tom unfurled the scroll, and he and Elenna both gaped at the yellowed parchment. It was completely blank.

"I was going to say any map is better than no map," Elenna said. "But in this case, I'm not so sure."

"It's all we have, sadly," Daltec said. "The map was made by the Wizard Zarlo – a strange fellow even before he vanished. He went to the Netherworld long ago. He did return, but disappeared again not long after, leaving this map behind in his study. I'm afraid this parchment is as changeable as the Wizard Zarlo's moods once were."

Bemused, Tom rolled the parchment up and tucked it into his tunic. Then he and Elenna turned to stand side by side in front of the portal. Tom felt a pang of worry to be leaving both Tangala and Avantia unguarded. But they had no choice. Four young heroes depended on him. He took a deep breath, and together, he and Elenna stepped into the mist.

4

THE VOICE OF ZARLO

Tom staggered as a strong, icy wind slammed into him, searing through his clothes and snatching away his breath. Beside him, Elenna gasped at the sudden cold. She pulled her cloak tightly about herself, then glanced around, frowning.

"What a dismal place!" she

shouted. They were standing at the base of a sheer cliff made from glassy black rock. The bright sun had vanished, replaced with a strange purple twilight, and the sky was the bruised, ominous violet of an impending storm. A craggy expanse of barren black stone stretched ahead of them, all the way to the distant horizon. Deep ravines scored the shiny rock as if rivers had once flowed across the terrain. But nothing else broke the monotony of the desolate landscape. No grass. No trees. No life at all.

Tom shuddered. "Let's find our missing candidates and get out of here as quickly as we can," he said.

"Hey! You out there!" a sharp voice piped up. It seemed to come from close by, but was strangely muffled. Tom stared about, looking for the speaker, but he and Elenna were utterly alone.

"You can't just stand around gawping, you know," the voice went on. "This place is dangerous!"

"Tom…" Elenna said, pointing at his chest. "The map!"

"Of course!" Tom said, drawing the parchment out.

"She's got her wits about her, that one!" the voice cackled, far more clearly now. Tom unrolled the map. "That's better," the voice said. "I am the Wizard Zarlo. Or at least I was

before I got myself stuck in this map. Ha! Should have used my eyeglass when I read the spell! Anyway, no one knows this terrain better than I do. You shouldn't be here. But since you are, listen up."

Tom and Elenna exchanged a wide-eyed glance. Tom had seen many strange things, but a talking map was new, even to him.

"Go on," the voice from the map

continued. "Ask me something."

Tom cleared his throat, remembering Daltec's warning about Zarlo's moods. "I have heard of your great knowledge regarding the Netherworld," Tom said. He felt foolish trying to flatter a map, but went on anyway. "We were hoping you could show us the way?"

"I can," Zarlo said. "But I'm not sure I should. It would be far safer for you to just leave now."

"We'd be very grateful to you," Elenna said. "Our friends are being held here against their will, by the Evil Wizard Malvel. We know they are being guarded by Beasts, so if you could show us how to locate them, that would be a great help."

Zarlo laughed, a harsh, grating sound. "And they call *me* mad!" he said. "Of course, I am mad – but not nearly as crazy as you two. Out looking for Beasts and Evil Wizards? Putting your lives at risk on a whim? Utter madness! Still…it's a long while since anyone asked for my help…"

Tom suddenly noticed dark lines and squiggles forming on the blank page in his hands. Glancing up at the landscape, Tom saw the lines more or less corresponded with the valleys and crevasses ahead. A dull purple smudge of light started to pulse on the map, nestled into the crook of a valley.

"Is that the nearest Beast?" Tom

asked. But before Zarlo could answer, a sharp gust of wind tugged at the map, almost snatching it away. The gust was followed by a high, piercing shriek. Tom glanced up to see a flock of Janus birds swoop over the cliff edge above and throw back their wings, diving in tight formation. Fear jolted through Tom as dozens of cruel beaks and rending talons knifed towards him and Elenna at deadly speed.

"Looks like you've made some enemies," Zarlo said, cheerfully. "Told you this place was bad!"

"But we only took one feather!" Elenna said.

"This is Malvel's doing," Tom said. "Run!" He shoved the parchment into his tunic and sprinted away with Elenna right behind him. Together they pounded over the rocky ground, jumping boulders and leaping gullies. Each time Tom glanced back, he saw more birds joining the flock, forming a vast, inky cloud. And the birds were getting closer by the moment...

Suddenly Elenna let out a yelp. Tom turned to see she had fallen behind, and then stumbled. *No!* He doubled back, running towards her, reaching out a hand... but before Elenna could rise, the birds dive-bombed towards her, blocking Tom's way, hiding her from sight.

Elenna screamed. Tom could just make out her shadowy form at the heart of the flock, slapping the birds away, shaking her head wildly as they tore clumps from her short hair and stabbed at her face.

Before Tom could reach his friend, the birds fastened their beaks and talons on Elenna's clothes and began to flap their wings, rising into the sky.

"Get off me!" Elenna cried. Tom caught sight of her wide, horrified eyes as the ground fell away below her. Fury boiled inside him.

"You let her go!" he shouted. Then,

calling on
the power of
his golden
boots and
leg armour
together, he
leapt upwards
with magical
speed. Tom
somersaulted
in the air, swinging his sword in
wide arcs around his friend, forcing
the birds to flee. Finally, he dropped
to the ground, landing neatly on
his feet. Elenna landed beside
him. Together they beat the last few
clinging, squawking birds from her
tunic and hair.

"Thank you!" Elenna said
breathlessly. Her face was ashen,
and blood ran from scratches on her
forehead and cheeks.

Tom shuddered. "That was a close
call," he said. "Let's be on our guard.
Malvel is clearly expecting us."

Tom and Elenna set off again,
trudging onwards over the lonely,
wind-blasted terrain. They scanned
the lifeless rock all around them
as they went, but the Janus birds
didn't return. Nothing stirred under
the purple sky except the howling,
mournful wind.

With no sun, and few landmarks
to navigate by, Tom soon drew out
Zarlo's map.

"Hello," Zarlo said. "Not given up yet, then?"

"Not while there's blood in my veins," Tom said.

Zarlo cackled. "Quite mad!" he said.

Tom soon found it wasn't easy to plot a course even using the map. The lines shifted and blurred. To make matters worse, Zarlo kept randomly chanting nonsense rhymes and breaking into song.

"Quiet!" Elenna hissed at the map. "We want to find the Beasts, not have them find us."

Zarlo sniffed. "I can't be expected to work in silence!" he snapped.

The rocky ground rose and fell as they travelled, but every new vista was as empty and barren as the last. They skirted around huge, smooth slabs of stone that jutted from the landscape like giant tombstones and scrambled over mounds of sharp, loose scree that cut their knees and hands.

In the constant, unnatural twilight, it was impossible to keep track of time, but Tom felt as if they had been travelling for ever. His legs ached and his throat was parched. He didn't dare drink more than small sips of water, because there might be no way to refill their supplies.

Elenna gasped and abruptly pulled up.

Tom followed the line of her gaze, his blood running cold when he saw they were nearing the edge of a precipice. Ahead, a rocky slope fell sharply downwards into a valley that was shrouded in thick mist. But Tom quicky realised it wasn't the almost sheer drop that had made Elenna gasp. It was something far more gruesome. The slope was littered with giant bones. Shredded tatters of mist wove through the horrible debris, and the wind moaned and sighed like mourners at a grave.

Brilliant white, or yellowed with age, the bones seemed almost luminous against the black of the rock. Some looked like scattered fragments of ancient carcasses – ribcages and horned skulls; limb bones with no body in sight. Other skeletons were almost complete. Tom saw the hollow remains of a huge snake with its mouth still wide open – as if ready to swallow its prey, even in death.

"What is this place?" Elenna asked.

"A graveyard for Beasts," Tom said. "And according to Zarlo's map, the Beast we're tracking isn't far."

They started off down the slope together. Tom climbed slowly and carefully, listening for any sound of a Beast as he went. Elenna clambered at his side, picking her way between the grisly remains. A pebble shifted under Tom's boot and clattered loudly away. He stopped, his heart in his mouth, listening.

"Is someone there?" a wavering voice suddenly cried. It sounded fearful and young, and familiar... "If anyone is out there, please help! I'm trapped."

"We're coming!" Elenna called back. They picked up their speed, half skidding on the slippery scree, and soon reached the valley floor. No wind stirred in the sheltered ravine, and the mist hung in cold, heavy curtains that clung to Tom's hair and clothes.

"Hello?" the voice called again, closer now. Tom slipped his sword from its sheath and crept onwards. Pale, shadowy forms loomed from the fog. Claws and fangs appeared suddenly, making Tom's pulse race. But each time he brandished his sword, he found himself staring at something long dead: a giant, shattered jawbone; the curled and wizened foot of a dragon with each claw still in place. There was death all around him.

"Where are you?" Elenna called.

"I'm here!" the voice said, muffled by the fog, but very nearby. Tom stepped from a bank of dense, swirling mist to see the biggest skull

yet, right in front of him. It had the curved fangs of a vast dog or wolf, and through the gaps between the skull's teeth, he could see a long-limbed boy crouching inside, trapped.

"Nolan!" Elenna said. "Are you hurt?"

Lifting his sword, Tom ran his eyes over the massive skull, looking for places where the bone was thinner. "Don't worry, we'll have you out of there in no time!" he told the boy. He raised his sword, ready to smash his way through.

"Wait!" the boy shouted. "Stay back. You don't understand. It's—" Nolan started to say something else, but his words were drowned out by a horrible grating, clanking sound that made Tom's hair stand on end.

"Tom, watch out!" Elenna cried. Tom sprang back just in time to see the massive skull lurch upwards, two flames igniting in the hollows of its eyes. Giant vertebrae held it aloft, and more bones were falling into place – shoulder blades… ribs. The Beast was coming to life.

And Nolan was trapped inside it!

5

MALVEL'S MARK

The giant skull seemed to leer
at Tom and Elenna as it hung before
them, huge teeth bared in a horrible
parody of a grin. The twin flames
in the pits of its eyes flickered like
candles, then suddenly flared bright.
Tom could just make out Nolan
hunched up inside the skull, without
even room to swing his scythe.

A low scraping sound echoed from the mist all around Tom, sending an icy shiver down his spine. He stared into the swirling whiteness and spotted several more bones sliding towards the skeleton and clunking into place. Legs…claws…a long, whip-like tail. Tom's skin crawled with horror. Elenna aimed an arrow at the skull.

"Help!" Nolan shouted, panic sounding in his voice for the first time. "Don't leave me here!"

"We're not going anywhere!" Tom called. "We'll get you out!" *But how?*

Elenna shook her head and lowered her bow. "There are too many gaps in the skeleton. I'm more likely to hit the boy than harm the Beast!"

In the muffled quiet of the swirling mist, the skeleton was unfolding itself slowly as it came together, still wearing its silent grin. And it was massive – bigger than a house. Tom knew it would be hard enough to

fight a Beast that size on any terms.
But this Beast had no flesh. Nothing
for a sword or an arrow to pierce.
It has no heart, Tom thought. *But
maybe it has a mind…*

He put a hand to the red jewel in
his belt. "Let the boy go," Tom told
the skeleton. He knew the Beast
would hear his thoughts, but he
spoke out loud so Nolan would hear
too.

The Beast let out a long, weary
sigh, like the dead air escaping
from a tomb. *Why should I fight
you, tiny human?* the skeleton
said. The Beast's voice was a rattling
echo in Tom's mind: ancient bones
knocking together in the darkness

of a grave. *I already have my prey. I am Ossiron the Fleshless Killer and I could snap you up in one bite – you and your little friend.*

Tom took a pace towards the gigantic skeleton – Ossiron. He noticed a mark between the creature's eyes. A black handprint. *Could that be Malvel's mark?* Tom wondered. *Could the Beast be enchanted?*

Tom fixed his gaze on the twin flames the jackal had for eyes. *You're nothing but a pile of old, dusty bones*, he told the Beast. *I don't think you can hurt me at all!*

A rattling sound started up, coming from the vast skeleton. Tom quickly realised what it was. Ossiron was shaking with rage, his bones clanking together as his fury built. Which was just what Tom wanted…

"What are you waiting for?" Tom shouted. "Aren't you going to eat me?" The Beast's eyes blazed brighter. Then, just as Tom thought the skeleton might shake himself to pieces, Ossiron opened his colossal jaws and let out a furious roar.

"Jump!" Tom shouted. Nolan was ready. The boy bent his knees and flung himself out from between the Beast's giant teeth. Cramped from being still for so long, Nolan landed in a clumsy heap, but Elenna was at

his side in an instant.

"See that he's unharmed," Tom
told her. "Keep an eye out for Malvel
and the other contestants. I'll deal
with Ossiron!"

The Beast glowered down at Tom,
deep orange flames flickering where
his eyes should be. Tom swallowed

hard. Each of the Beast's razor-sharp teeth were longer than Tom's arm and the honed claws that tipped the jackal's massive feet looked sharp enough to tear out Tom's heart. Ossiron let out a rumbling growl. *Either you give me back my meal, or you shall take its place!* he told Tom.

"I don't think so," Tom said, keeping his tone light and taunting despite the fear that squeezed his gut. "Why should I be afraid of you?"

This is why! With a furious roar, Ossiron lunged, his jaws opening wide. Tom's heart hammered as if it might burst, but he held his ground, blasted by the Beast's deafening cry until the last possible moment. Then he neatly danced aside. *SNAP!* The gigantic teeth slammed shut, closing on nothing but mist.

You will die! Ossiron boomed, swiping for Tom with an immense clawed foot. Tom dived out of reach, feeling the massive claws swish through the air right behind him, then he spun and leapt towards the jackal's leg, hacking at the bone with his sword,

chopping a gouge.

Ossiron shuddered with rage and let out a long, low growl – a deep rumble that made the ground shake. And with the sound, a cloud of dark maroon-coloured smoke started to pour from the Beast's open mouth.

Tom's eyes blurred as the fumes hit him. He almost gagged at the stench of carrion – putrid and rotten. The smoke caught in Tom's throat, making him cough and choke. More smoke poured from the Beast's mouth, swirling out over the valley, engulfing Tom and everything else, making it impossible to see. Gasping, Tom tore a length of fabric from his tunic and tied it over his mouth and nose. He heard fabric rip as Elenna and Nolan hurriedly did the same. Tom peered into the mist, but he couldn't see anything – not even his own feet. He strained his ears, listening for the telltale sound of giant claws creeping over rock, but everything was deathly, eerily quiet.

"NO!" Elenna suddenly shouted. Tom heard the clatter of booted feet and a high, angry scream.

"Take that!" Nolan shouted, his voice cracking with fury. Tom heard the *thwack* of a blade slamming into bone – then a roar from Ossiron, the loudest one yet.

Using the sound to guide him, Tom

struck off through the smoke at a run, leaping bones as they loomed in his path, desperate to reach Nolan before the boy came to harm. Tom could see shadowy movement ahead – the Beast's huge white skeleton,

just visible through the churning red darkness. Ossiron was thrashing his forelimb from side to side trying to dislodge something. *Nolan!* The boy had driven his scythe into Ossiron's leg and was holding tight to the hilt.

He's brave, Tom thought, *but bravery won't keep him alive.* As the putrid smoke closed in once again, Tom raced on. *I have to save him!*

6

BLIND PURSUIT

Tom clambered through the vile red-brown smoke, stumbling over the broken remains that littered the ground, listening for the sound of the Beast's rattle and clank, but the rank fumes seemed to deaden all sound. Tom couldn't hear anything – not even a whimper from Nolan. But he wouldn't let himself think about what that meant. He wouldn't imagine the boy lying lifeless in a graveyard of Beasts...

Tom shook his head, trying to clear the dizzy sickness that rolled over him in waves. Weak and nauseous, he could barely lift his feet, but he kept going, casting about in the near-darkness. *I won't give up on him!* Suddenly, a pale shape emerged from the smoke. Tom swung his sword, but just in time, he realised it was Elenna. Her eyes looked huge above her mask, and she had an arrow aimed at Tom's heart.

"I thought you were the Beast!" they both said at once.

"Have you seen Nolan?" Elenna asked, lowering her bow. "He wanted to help defeat Ossiron. I couldn't stop him."

"It's not your fault," Tom said. "I should have guessed he'd do that. After all, he wants to be Master of the Beasts. He's brave, and has a good aim too! He actually managed to stab Ossiron, but I lost him in all this smoke." Tom hoped with all his heart that Nolan's brave act hadn't been his last.

"We had better split up to look for him," Elenna said. "I'll go left, you go right. Shout if you find him." Tom nodded, and they both set off into the cloying smoke.

Tom hurried onward, covering as much ground as he could, staring into the maroon darkness so hard his eyes burned. Even with the fabric covering his mouth and nose, the fumes crept into his throat, making his breath rasp and his lungs sting. The smoke seemed to be getting thicker. It felt almost like pushing through something half-solid. His head was spinning.

Then the ground dropped away beneath Tom's feet. He tried to catch his balance but toppled forward, rolling over and over, sharp rock biting into his flesh as he tumbled. When Tom finally came to rest, he was lying at the bottom of a ravine. The Beast's evil-smelling smoke hadn't reached the valley floor, but mist still hung in white tatters over the inky rock. Every part of Tom throbbed with pain as he heaved himself up. He had bruises and grazes everywhere, but nothing seemed to be broken. His heart clenched as he spotted a body lying still nearby. *Nolan!* Fearing the worst, Tom hurried to the boy.

Nolan had a deep

gash on his forehead, but his eyes
flickered open at the sound of Tom's
approach. The boy pushed himself
up to sitting and picked up his
scythe.

"I can still fight," Nolan said.

Tom was about to thank the
boy for all he'd done so far, but
a horrible, spiteful laugh echoed
around them.

"Fools!" Malvel's voice rang out
clearly, but Tom couldn't pinpoint
it. It was as if the Dark Wizard
was everywhere at once. "You have
failed, Tom! I have waited too long
for freedom. I won't allow you
to take it from me. You and your
protégés might be brave, but I have

twice defeated death. This time, I will have my revenge on Avantia, and Tangala too."

"I have to fight Malvel," Tom told Nolan. "And I need to find the other three candidates. I want to send you home, to the palace."

Nolan shook his head. "But I can help you!" he said. "I wounded the Beast. I can do it again."

"I don't doubt that," Tom said, resting a hand on the younger boy's shoulder. "And I do need your help. I need someone I can trust to take word to Daltec and Rotu, back in Pania." Tom hurriedly took the purple jewel from its place in his belt, then he closed his eyes and pictured the throne room, back at the palace in Tangala. When he opened his eyes, the purple stone had started to throb with light. Tom traced a glowing circle on a nearby rock with the jewel... then as he joined the two ends, he held his breath... *I hope this works!* The instant Tom completed the circle, the dark rock inside vanished, replaced with a view of Rotu's breakfast room. Tom could see a table laden with fresh bread, pastries and fruit. Nolan gaped in astonishment, peering at the food and rich fabrics beyond the portal.

"That's amazing!" he said.

It wasn't the room Tom had

intended, but it would do. Before Nolan could argue, Tom shoved the boy into the portal, which closed after him, leaving Tom alone in the misty darkness.

Tom clicked the purple jewel back into his belt. The lifeless black stone all around him seemed even grimmer after his brief glimpse of the palace, but Tom put that from his mind.

"Tom!" Elenna called from somewhere above him. "I heard voices. Where are you?"

"I'm coming up!" Tom called back. Then he straightened his spine, drawing together all his courage and strength. *Time to put an end to the Beast!*

BAIT

Tom hauled himself up the cliff face, his bruised muscles protesting at each movement and the sharp rock cutting into his hands. As he climbed higher, tendrils of smoke wafted over him, making his head swim and bile rise in his throat. He was soon clammy with sweat despite the cold. Finally, he could see Elenna above him, peering over the cliff edge. He forced himself up the last stretch, then gratefully took the hand she offered him.

"I sent Nolan home," he told Elenna once he'd clambered up on to solid

ground. "He didn't want to go, but at least he's safe now, and we know that as long as we have my purple jewel, we can get the rest of the candidates home."

"What about Ossiron?" Elenna asked.

"I think Malvel's enchanted him," Tom said. "Which means we have to defeat him. We can't leave him under the wizard's control."

"I can hear him out there," Elenna said. "Listen!"

Tom did as Elenna asked, gazing into the dense haze all around them. It was impossible to see anything, but Tom could definitely hear the distant clatter and clunk of Ossiron's bony steps.

"Let's see if we can get him to come to us," Tom said. Resting his hand on the red jewel in his belt, he called to the Beast with his mind. *Are you out there, Ossiron?* he asked. *Why don't you come and fight? Or are you sulking because I've sent your prey away? Nolan's safe and sound back in Tangala now. If you want human flesh, it will have to be me!*

Tom heard a low growl, followed by the hollow rattle of bones clanking together, rapidly getting louder.

"He's coming," Elenna whispered, aiming an arrow into the fog. Tom braced himself, ready for the attack.

ROOOAAAAR! Ossiron's massive skull burst from the churning smoke. Elenna fired one arrow, then another, before leaping aside. Tom swung his sword. He just managed to swipe a blow across the jackal's temple, but Ossiron ploughed on, slamming his vast head into Tom's shoulder, sending him flying. Tom crashed down on his back and slid to a stop, coming to rest right at the edge of the cliff face he'd just climbed up. Ossiron roared, and a moment later, Elenna landed heavily at Tom's side.

Winded and bruised, they both eased themselves up to sitting. "Maybe using ourselves as bait isn't such a great plan!" Elenna said.

"That's it!" Tom said, her words giving him a sudden idea. "We need bait!"

"I'm fairly sure that's the opposite of what I just said..." Elenna muttered, frowning.

"Not us!" Tom said, drawing Zarlo's map from his pocket. "This!"

Elenna grinned. "It might just work."

"What? What will work? What's going on?" Zarlo asked, his voice becoming clearer as Tom unrolled the parchment.

"We were just wondering if you could sing us one of your songs," Elenna said.

"I suppose I could," Zarlo said. "Let me see. I'll have to think of something suitable…"

Tom set Zarlo's map on the ground, near the cliff edge, then mimed for Elenna to be quiet. As they both tiptoed away, Tom could hear Zarlo chanting something. He frowned as he recognised the tune, and Elenna rolled her eyes. Zarlo was singing about cake, a merry song normally sung at children's parties. Tom could also hear the sound of dry bones pacing over rock. He and Elenna crouched down, waiting, their eyes on the fog.

They didn't need to wait for long. Ossiron bounded from the mist, eyes blazing and jaws wide open. Tom sprang into action. Racing over the uneven ground, he swung his sword in a long, low double-handed arc as Ossiron hurtled past. *THWACK!* The blade severed the Beast's clawed foot.

Ossiron howled with rage, but the momentum of his attack kept him going. The jackal shot over the edge of the cliff and plummeted, landing with a mighty *crash!*

Tom called on the power of his golden boots, ready to leap on to the Beast from above and finish what he had started. But before he could jump, the Beast's long tail swiped through the air. Tom tried to dodge, but there was no time. The bony tail whacked Tom across the back so hard his vision blanked with pain, and he was catapulted forward over the edge of the cliff. For the second time, Tom tumbled into the valley, his bruised body hitting sharp

outcrops all
the way down.
Crack! His head
slammed hard
against the
valley floor.

Tom groaned
and rolled over,
gasping with
agony, only to
find himself
staring up into Ossiron's blazing
eyes.

Now I will finish you! the Beast
growled. Tom lifted his shield, but he
knew it couldn't save him. The Beast
would swallow him and his shield
together in one bite.

ETERNAL SLEEP

As Tom lay, winded and battered, staring up into the jackal-Beast's smouldering gaze, he thought of the three young candidates still lost in the Netherworld. *Miandra, Katya and Rafe. I've failed them!*

Ossiron's eyes flashed hungrily. His vast teeth parted, and his jaws stretched wide…

Suddenly, Tom heard a loud, sharp whistle from above him.

"Over here, you great lump!" Elenna shouted. With a snarl, Ossiron swung his huge muzzle around, away from Tom. Craning his neck, Tom could see Elenna standing at the clifftop, silhouetted against the purple sky, her bow aimed and ready.

"Come on!" Elenna called to the Beast. "Finish me off before I pierce you full of arrows like a pincushion. Or I could put one through your eye socket. How would you like that?" With Ossiron distracted, Tom heaved himself up. The Beast's spine rose like a staircase before him, and Tom suddenly had a plan. He only hoped Elenna could keep Ossiron distracted for just a bit longer.

Calling on the strength of heart of his golden chainmail, Tom leapt on to the tip of the colossal Beast's tail and began to climb. He could still  hear Elenna taunting the Beast – saying something about air where a brain should be... Leaping from

vertebra to vertebra, Tom quickly
made it up on to the Beast's broad
back. But then Ossiron suddenly
stiffened. Tom froze, his gut
tightening with fear. *He must be
able to feel me...* The Beast let out
a furious growl. Tom dropped to his
knees and held tight to Ossiron's
spine just as the Beast started to
buck wildly. Tom's teeth clashed
together, and his arms were almost
pulled from their sockets, but he
managed to keep his grip.

Get off! I will destroy you! the
Beast growled, shaking furiously,
trying to dislodge Tom. Still
gripping with his hands and
knees, Tom began climbing once

more. It was like trying to climb a ship's mast in a storm – but Tom knew this was his last chance. He clambered on, reaching the Beast's broad shoulders.

Ossiron turned his vast head, trying to snap at Tom, but his neck wouldn't reach, and his teeth clashed on empty air. Tom scrambled higher, pulling himself on to the narrower bones of the jackal's neck.

This has to work…

Summoning every scrap of strength he could muster, Tom raised himself up, lifted his sword and called on the magical skills of his golden gauntlets. *THWACK!* He

smashed his blade down between
two brittle vertebrae, right at the
point where bone linked to bone.

ROARRR! Ossiron gave a mighty
shudder, pitching Tom forward.
But, clinging with his knees and
straddling the Beast's neck, Tom

somehow kept his seat. He sent his blade slamming down once more. *CHOP!* Sharp metal hacked through bone, severing Ossiron's mighty head.

As Ossiron's skull crashed down on to the valley floor, Tom called on the power of his golden boots and leapt after it, throwing himself clear of the remains of the skeleton.

Landing beside the Beast's huge skull, Tom turned just in time to see the rest of the skeleton slump to the ground like a pile of sticks. Bones rolled and clattered away in every direction, tumbling over the rocky ground. But eventually the valley fell silent. The mist billowed and began to clear. Tugging the makeshift mask from his face, Tom circled the Beast's fallen skull until he could look Ossiron in the eyes. Malvel's handprint had vanished. The flames in the Beast's eyes were dim now – barely more than flickering candles.

Tom put his own hand on the pale bone of Ossiron's skull and at the same time, touched the red jewel in his belt. *You are defeated*, Tom told the Beast. *Now you can rest.*

The Beast let out a heavy sigh. *Rest?* he asked bitterly, his voice a tired rasp in Tom's mind. *My eternal rest should never have been broken. Humans were never meant to come to this place. You bring Evil!*

I am here to defeat Evil, Tom told the jackal.

Then I wish you luck, Ossiron said. With that, the Beast heaved his longest sigh yet, and the flames of his eyes guttered and snuffed out.

Sleep well, Tom told the Beast, feeling a stab of pity.

"You did it!" Elenna said, skidding to a halt at the bottom of the valley with Zarlo's map in her hand.

Tom smiled. "*We* did it," he corrected her. "You made excellent bait in the end!"

"Bait!" Zarlo's voice piped up from the map Elenna was holding. "I can't believe you used me to lure the

Beast! Of all the dirty tricks! And to think it was fooled! Mistaking me for you two bunglers!"

"It worked, didn't it?" Tom said, taking the map from Elenna and running his eyes over it. "And there isn't a speck of damage to the map, which hopefully means you can help us find the next Beast..."

Zarlo sniffed. "Hmmm. If you say sorry, I suppose I will try!"

Tom and Elenna both exchanged a smile. "We really are sorry," they said.

Tom was pleased to see faint lines forming on the map he was holding. But suddenly, a shadow fell over them from above.

Tom glanced up. Hanging above

the valley, seated on a chariot of bone held aloft by a flock of Janus birds, was Malvel.

"You haven't won!" Malvel cried. "Ossiron was a puppy compared to what I have in store for you!"

His jaw tightening with anger, Tom lifted his sword and pointed it towards the Dark Wizard. Elenna fitted an arrow to her bow and aimed.

"I give you one last chance to release your captives!" Tom called.

Malvel let out a sharp cackle of laughter and brandished the *Book of Derthsin.* "You are in no position to be making demands, boy!" the wizard said. "This is my realm, with my Beasts and my rules. You should have given me the purple jewel while you had the chance! Now it will be my pleasure to prise it from your dead body!"

With an angry growl, Elenna let her arrow fly. But the Janus birds were too quick. They flapped higher, carrying Malvel out of reach, and the arrow sailed through empty sky.

"Good riddance!" Elenna snapped.

Tom turned his gaze back to the parchment he was holding. A purple dot now pulsed steadily on the map. "We have three more competitors to rescue," Tom told Elenna. "This Quest has only just begun."

THE END

CONGRATULATIONS, YOU HAVE COMPLETED THIS QUEST!

At the end of each chapter you were
awarded a special gold coin.
The QUEST in this book was
worth an amazing 8 coins.

Look at the Beast Quest totem picture
opposite to see how far you've come
in your journey to become

MASTER OF THE BEASTS.

The more books you read,
the more coins you will collect!

Do you want your own
Beast Quest Totem?

1. Cut out and collect the coin below
2. Go to the Beast Quest website
3. Download and print out your totem
4. Add your coin to the totem

www.beastquest.co.uk

READ THE BOOKS, COLLECT THE COINS!
EARN COINS FOR EVERY CHAPTER YOU READ!

550+

515

480

445

550+ COINS
MASTER OF THE BEASTS

410

410 COINS
HERO

395

380

365

350

320

350 COINS
WARRIOR

290

260

230

230 COINS
KNIGHT

217

206

191

180

180 COINS
SQUIRE

146

112

78

44

44 COINS
PAGE

30

19

8

8 COINS
APPRENTICE

READ ALL THE BOOKS IN SERIES 28:
THE NETHERWORLD!

*Don't miss the next
exciting Beast Quest
book: STYX THE
LURKING TERROR!*

*Read on for a sneak
peek…*

THE DARKEST
NIGHT

Tom drew the last fragment of bread
from the pouch at his belt. It was
stale and so small it would barely
take the edge off his hunger. Still, he
took a small bite, washing it down
with a sip from his flask. He had to

tip the waterskin right back to reach the gritty dregs at the bottom.

"I'm almost out of water," Tom told Elenna. She sat opposite him, her knees drawn up under her chin, hugging herself to keep warm.

"My flask's almost empty too," she said, through chattering teeth. "We'll need to find more soon. And I wish we had wood for a campfire. Or even a branch to make a torch. It's so cold!"

Tom rubbed at his arms and legs, trying to shift the bone-aching chill that had leached into them while sleeping on the rocky ground. Beyond Elenna, he could see nothing but blackness. They had stopped only briefly to recover from their battle with the jackal-Beast, Ossiron. In that short time, night had fallen in the Netherworld, turning the air bitterly cold.

"We'll warm up as soon as we start moving again," Tom said, drawing a map from inside his tunic. With no moon or stars, it was their only way of navigating through the strange, gloomy realm. Unfortunately, the map had a voice and a mind of its own – that of Zarlo. *Can we really trust a wizard careless enough to get stuck inside his own map?* Tom wondered. Then he sighed. They had little choice.

"Still not given up, then?" Zarlo

asked chirpily as Tom unfurled the parchment.

"You know we can't do that," Tom said. "Not while three more innocent lives depend on us." Tom and Elenna were on a Quest to rescue four young candidates for the title of Tangala's new Master of the Beasts. They had been kidnapped by Malvel, Tom's oldest enemy. The Evil Wizard had transported the contestants to the Netherworld, hoping to bargain their lives for his freedom. Tom and Elenna had already rescued a brave lad called Nolan, but three other young hopefuls remained lost in the realm, guarded by Beasts.

"So you keep telling me," Zarlo

said. "But something's been bothering me. Surely this wizard, Marvin or Malvin or whatever his name is, can't  really be that dangerous. I've never even heard of him."

Tom frowned, baffled. *Everyone's heard of Malvel! How long has Zarlo been trapped in this map?*

"Believe me," Tom said, "he's dangerous. He's probably the most powerful wizard ever to have lived."

Zarlo sniffed. "He got trapped here in the Netherworld, didn't he? *I* didn't have any problems travelling here at all."

"Hmm," Elenna said. "Apart from the one slight problem of getting yourself stuck inside a map. How did that happen again?"

"Bah! Not through lack of power, I can assure you," Zarlo said. "It was a simple mistake in the words of a spell. A mispronunciation, if you like. Could have happened to anyone. Now, do you want some help or are you just going to ask foolish questions? I seem to recall you said something about fire…"

Before Tom could argue, Zarlo

muttered a few strange, guttural words, and a green fire sizzled into life on the ground between Tom and Elenna. Flames licked up towards Zarlo's map, singeing the edges. Tom whipped the parchment out of the way before it caught light.

"Oops! Bit of a close one there!" Zarlo said. "That's the trouble with being so powerful. It's a risky business. Which is why I can assure you, Malvel can't possibly be as powerful as I am...or...er...was..."

"You might be right," Tom said, knowing it was best to keep the wizard happy. "But Malvel's got a book of spells that you must have heard of. The *Book of Derthsin*?"

"Derthsin? The name does ring a bell," said Zarlo thoughtfully. "Remind me."

Tom took a deep breath, doing his best to stay patient though he was desperate to get moving. "Derthsin was an ancient Evil sorcerer who controlled Beasts with magic. He could also change the landscape around him – turn air to fire, earth to water, raise mountains from plains, change jungle to desert. Now that Malvel has Derthsin's book, he'll be able to use all these powerful spells."

"Interesting," Zarlo muttered. "Very interesting…"

Frustration welled inside Tom but before he could snap at Zarlo, Elenna grabbed his arm, pointing to

the starless sky. "Look!" Tom saw a
darker blot of black sweep overhead,
then heard a high, thin screech.

Read
STYX THE LURKING TERROR
to find out what happens next!

Don't miss the
thrilling new series
from Adam Blade!

FROM THE CREATOR OF BeastQuest
ADAM BLADE

SPACE
WARS

CURSE OF THE ROBO-DRAGON

31901068287673